PERFECT PANCAKES
·*if you please*·

WILLIAM WISE ◆ *pictures by* RICHARD EGIELSKI

Dial Books for Young Readers *New York*

Published by Dial Books for Young Readers
A Division of Penguin Books USA Inc.
375 Hudson Street
New York, New York 10014
Text copyright © 1997 by William Wise
Pictures copyright © 1997 by Richard Egielski
All rights reserved
Designed by Atha Tehon
Printed in Hong Kong
First Edition
1 3 5 7 9 10 8 6 4 2

Library of Congress Cataloging in Publication Data
Wise, William, date
Perfect pancakes if you please/ by William Wise;
pictures by Richard Egielski.—1st ed.
p. cm.
Summary: King Felix loves pancakes so much that he offers his daughter's
hand in marriage to the man who can make the perfect pancake.
ISBN 0-8037-1446-7 (trade).—ISBN 0-8037-1447-5 (library)
[1. Fairy tales. 2. Pancakes, waffles, etc.—Fiction.
3. Cookery—Fiction. 4. Kings, queens, rulers, etc.—Fiction.]
I. Egielski, Richard, ill. II. Title.
PZ8.W7535Pe 1997 [E]—dc20 95-32322 CIP AC

*The illustrations were created with watercolor
and gouache on watercolor paper.*

For Elizabeth, a real princess
W.W.

There once was a greedy king who loved to eat pancakes. His name was Felix, and he loved them so much that he ate some for breakfast every day of the year.

Yet he was never satisfied—either his pancakes were too dry, or too buttery, or they had too much maple syrup on them and tasted too sweet.

So one morning King Felix issued a Royal Proclamation. In three months' time a contest would be held at the palace to see if any man in the kingdom could make him a stack of perfect pancakes. And if any man could, he would receive a prize—the king's only daughter, Princess Elizabeth, for his bride in marriage.

Outraged at this announcement, the princess marched off to see her mother, Queen Ursula. "This time my father has gone too far!" she cried. "Offering *me*, his only daughter, in exchange for a stack of pancakes!"

"Oh Lizzy, do simmer down," Queen Ursula said. "You know your father—he's simply wild about pancakes, and likes to think up different excuses for eating them. So this time it's a harmless contest that nobody will win. He'll get to eat all the pancakes he could possibly desire, and that will be that."

"But how can you be sure that nobody will win the contest?" the princess asked.

"Because," the queen replied, "there is no such thing in the world as a stack of *perfect* pancakes. It would take black magic itself to make such a thing."

"And nobody practices black magic in the kingdom?" the princess said.

"Not anymore, Lizzy. There used to be someone who was very, very good at it—Maximilian, the Evil Inventor, who lived on the other side of the mountains. But that was twenty years ago, and he was an old man then, so he's probably dead by now. *He* might have been able to pull it off—but there's nobody else."

"Well, you'd better be right about the contest," the princess said, "because *I* am not going to marry someone just because *he* can make a good pancake!"

"Of course you're not," said the queen. "You can marry whoever you like."

In three months' time the contest was held at the palace, and the princess was pleasantly surprised to discover that it was all quite entertaining. Men from every corner of the kingdom were there—preparing their pancakes in the Royal Kitchen and then presenting them to the king.

But as Queen Ursula had foreseen, none of their offerings satisfied her husband. King Felix ate stack after stack of the pancakes, and found them too dry, too buttery, or too sweet.

Toward the end of the contest, the princess spied a tall young stranger who was so handsome and charming, she fell in love with him on the spot. His name was Roderick, and he was a brilliant scientist who specialized in building long-distance balloons and other flying machines. But of course he didn't win the contest either—the king ate Roderick's pancakes and shook his head, just as he had with all of the others.

When King Felix had swallowed every last pancake in sight, he said, "Ah, what a pity—not one man in all my kingdom has made me a stack of perfect pancakes. And so I will not give away my only daughter as a bride."

Suddenly the door flew open, and a strange-looking old man shuffled into the throne room. He had a long white beard, mean yellowish eyes, and a nose that twitched with mischief. But the strangest thing about him was the little black box he pulled along behind him.

"Your Majesty," said the old man, "today I've brought you what you've always wanted—a stack of perfect pancakes!"

Everyone laughed at the stranger and his little black box, except the queen, who recognized him. "My dear," she said to the king, "you must have nothing to do with this creature! He is Maximilian, the Evil Inventor, who lives on the other side of the mountains. If you eat even one of his pancakes, it will lead to nothing but misfortune!"

"Nonsense!" said the king. "What harm can there be in sampling the man's pancakes?" Then he turned to the stranger and said, "Let's have a taste, shall we?"

The stranger pointed to the little black box. "You have only to press the white button," he said, "and a stack of perfect pancakes will appear a moment afterward. And whenever you like, just press the button again, and another stack will appear. The box will make pancakes forever, Your Majesty, and serve you for the rest of your days."

"Very well," the king said, and lo and behold, as soon as his finger touched the button . . .

the box went "Clip-Clop, Flip-Flop," and out came a stack of beautiful pancakes. Everyone gasped in alarm, for now they realized that the stranger was indeed Maximilian, the Evil Inventor. But the king didn't care. He smelled the pancakes and they smelled delicious.

"Well, they're not too dry," he said, letting the first mouthful melt on the end of his tongue. "And they're certainly not too buttery or too sweet. In fact, they're the only *perfect* pancakes I've ever eaten!"

He pushed the white button again, and again the box went "Clip-Clop, Flip-Flop," and out came another stack of pancakes.

King Felix ate the second stack, and several more. Then he patted his stomach happily and said to the inventor, "Your box makes nothing but perfect pancakes. So I will keep it, and you may have my daughter for your bride."

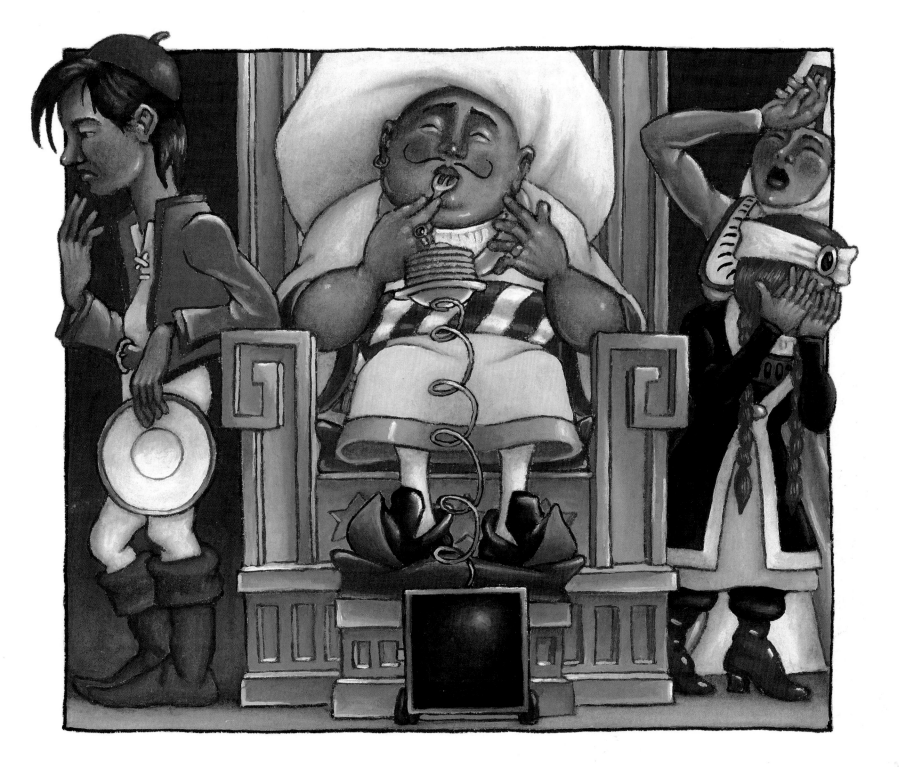

Hearing this, the princess became furious! "Marry *him*?" she cried. "Not in a million years!"

"You don't think you're being too hasty?" the king said. "He might be nicer than he *looks*. And I did make him a promise, you know."

"Then you'll simply have to *break* your promise," the princess said.

The king rubbed his chin and turned to Maximilian. "I'm afraid there's been a slight change in plans," he said. "You may not have my daughter for your bride, after all. But—in exchange for your little black box—I'm happy to offer you a bagful of diamonds, or a beautiful tapestry from my palace, or a hundred bars of pure gold!"

The inventor would not hear of it. "I won the contest," he shouted, "and I want nothing but the princess for my bride!"

"Well, you may want her," said the king, "but she won't have you."

"Very well," Maximilian said. "Keep her—and keep the box too. But because you broke your word, that box will be the ruin of your happiness!" And the Evil Inventor vanished from the room, leaving the little black box behind.

Just then a curious thing happened. Though nobody touched the white button, the little black box went "Clip-Clop, Flip-Flop," all by itself, and out came a stack of pancakes. "How strange!" the king said. "I wonder why it did that?"

Even as he spoke, the box went "Clip-Clop, Flip-Flop" again, and another stack of pancakes appeared.

Before long there were pancakes all over the room. The king began to eat them, and so did everyone else, but they couldn't keep up with the little black box.

By the next day the entire palace was filled with pancakes, and the king began to hate the very idea of them. "How happy I would be," he said, "if only that awful box would stop making them." But he knew of course that only Maximilian, the Evil Inventor, could make it stop. And he would never do that, unless the princess agreed to marry him.

When all hope seemed lost, who should rush up to the palace but Roderick, the handsome young scientist, to announce that he had just finished building an extraordinary new flying machine!

"Your Majesty," he said to the king, "let me put the little black box inside my machine, and send it off to the moon! There it will circle around forever, and down here we'll finally be rid of all these loathsome pancakes!"

King Felix eagerly agreed.

The box was rolled into the flying machine and fastened into place. But Maximilian, the Evil Inventor, soon learned of the plan. He knew that once the little black box disappeared into the heavens, any hope he still had of marrying the princess would be gone.

So when he thought no one was looking, he sneaked aboard the flying machine to steal back the box. And while he struggled to get it loose, the door was slammed shut behind him.

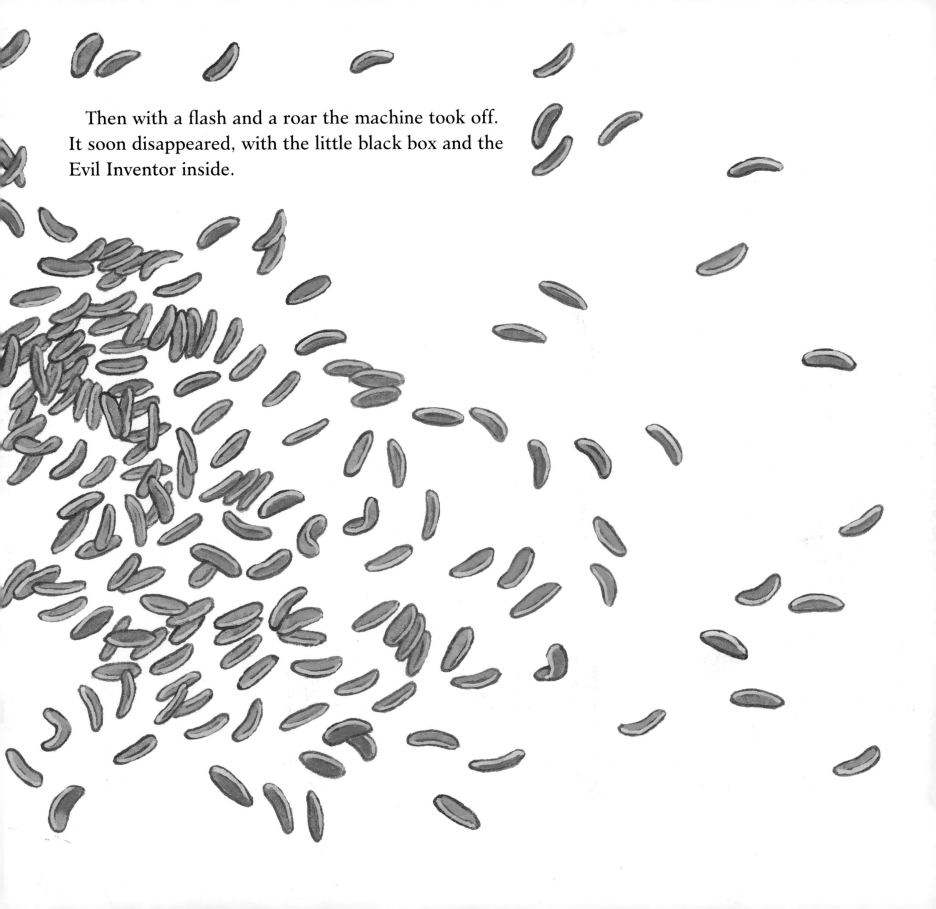

Then with a flash and a roar the machine took off. It soon disappeared, with the little black box and the Evil Inventor inside.

Roderick of course was a hero now. He declared his love to the princess, and a year later they were married. After that they lived happily in the palace with King Felix and Queen Ursula. There they had many feasts, parties, and banquets, but one thing was never served at any of them. Never did a stack of pancakes appear in the palace again—no, not a single one—and even greedy King Felix did not seem to miss them.

It is true that after a while he did begin to eat a good many *waffles*, but as they say in certain parts of the kingdom, that is really another story altogether.